All the Beautiful Boys

PUBLISHER'S CHOICE

A COLLECTION OF SLIM VOLUMES
SELECTED BY OUR PUBLISHER

No. 5

All the Beautiful Boys

AN ORIGINAL SHORT STORY FROM
THE MASTER OF QUEER BRITISH
HORROR WILLIAM JACKSON

Cambridge
Queer Press

First published in 2024 by the Cambridge Queer Press
an imprint of MFco Ltd. Unit 4 City Limits, Danehill, Reading
RG6 4UP, UK.

ISBN 978-1-912622-53-5

Copyright © Cambridge Queer Press 2024.
www.cambridgequeerpress.co.uk

Text is set in Cormorant Garamond 13pt on 19pt.

All the Beautiful Boys

His muscular arms broke the glassy surface; foam swelled and fizzled in his wake. His movement was pure and purposive, driving him swiftly through the water in a perfect line. As he approached the deep end of the pool, he pushed himself harder, increasing his speed, performed a half-somersault, stretching out his upper body, arms above his head, torpedo-like, and propelled himself sleekly back the way he had come. After ten more lengths, he climbed out of the pool, water beading and glistening against the v-shape of his sharply-defined shoulders and back. He peeled off his red swim briefs and took a long shower; dried and gelled his thick dark hair; pulled out of his kit bag a neatly folded white tee shirt. He liked the cool of the satiny material against his skin; he liked the way it lay taut across his powerful chest and biceps. As he walked to his car, he broke open a power bar; the gleaming XJ-S had been a sorry wreck six months ago but Joe had worked hard on the restoration. Now it was the envy of every boy-racer in the neighbourhood and he'd invested in two heavy-duty steering locks - just to be doubly sure. He checked his watch. The journey to Kenny's took about twenty minutes, less if the traffic was light. A black limousine was parked outside the apartment building when he arrived. Joe laughed, 'Have you won the lottery and forgotten to tell me?'

'Just get in,' Kenny said. 'You're in for the night of your life.' The uniformed chauffeur eased the car smoothly onto the main road.

'What's with the gold-star service?'

'Bastien does this for all his boys.'

'His boys?'

'Everyone who's invited to one of his parties. Honestly Joe, you're going to love it; the food is out of this world.'

The Mercedes seemed to glide on air as the early evening light softened and blurred. London planes gave way to faceless dual carriageway skirting now an industrial estate, now retail parks, now blocks of council flats. The sun had already dipped below the skyline when they arrived in South Kensington. The car drew up outside a large gothic revival mansion. Towering above the roof-line were eight ornately-decorated chimney stacks, puffing smoke like so many beagles. The house had beautiful mullioned windows and gargoyles snarling down from stepped gables; a high red-brick wall concealed the remainder of the structure, giving it a blueish, vaguely sinister air. Kenny marched up to the wrought iron gates with practised eagerness.

'This is a pretty grand place,' Joe said, grabbing Kenny's arm to slow his stride. 'Does this Bastien guy own it?'

'Sure does. He's minted.'

Joe considered what they were wearing: faded Levis, tee shirts, trainers. He was reminded of one of those dreams when you're running down the high street, buck naked. 'Aren't we a bit underdressed for a fancy do?'

'It's always very informal. Bastien says good food and good conversation are the only things that really matter.'

A footman led them from the panelled

hallway down a wide oak staircase and into the vast ballroom with serpentine walls and a domed ceiling decorated with elaborate plasterwork. The room was full of men, the majority about the same age as Kenny and Joe. Only a handful were older, chatting in a loose circle: mid-fifties, no more, Joe guessed. Waiters moved deftly through the crowd dispensing French Martinis, Negronis, or misted flutes of Pol Roger. Excited chatter filled the space. Kenny squeezed Joe's hand. 'Let's go and say 'hi' to our host.'

He was tall, attractive, holding court with a clique of eager young men. His refined manner was underlined by perfectly drawn features. His dark hair was flecked with grey and he wore a beautifully cut navy blue lounge suit. Joe recognised him from the men's glossies: he was Bastien Ricaud, a wealthy French industrialist with connections to some of the

most powerful men in Europe, Xavier Niel, François Pinault, Laurent Dassault and the rest.

'Kenneth has told me a lot about you, Joseph,' Bastien said. 'It's a pleasure to finally meet you.' His voice was a pure, warm baritone; Joe found it oddly charming that he called them both by their full names. He was quick to notice the young athletic man at Bastien's side - and that Bastien was holding his hand. The boy was introduced as Wayne Dillard, an American. Joe liked Wayne's square-jawed handsomeness, his beautiful skin with a sheen as if brushed with warm butter. Kenny whispered to Joe that Bastien was paying to put Wayne through college.

The other young men seemed less than delighted by the new additions to their little group. Joe imagined they all hoped one day to replace Wayne in Bastien's affections. But it turned out it was Joe who was getting all of the attention and he swelled with the pleasure of being in the spotlight. Bastien seemed to know a great deal about him already and was keen to find out more. What were his hobbies? What books had he read? What was his favourite food?

The dinner gong sounded: a lush trembling note, slow to die; and then two tall panelled doors swung open at the far end of the ballroom. Beyond was the dining hall with tables elegantly laid for six and eight. There were no name cards and momentarily the evening resembled an EasyJet scramble for seats. Joe stuck close to Bastien and sat down next to him; Wayne on Bastien's other side; Kenny hadn't been so lucky - or determined - and ended up several tables away. Now the room was full of white-gloved waiters, moving skillfully between the tables, trays held high: the service had begun.

First an *amuse bouche* of blinis glistening with beads of trout roe caviar and *crème fraiche*. Then Ballotine of duck liver. Next fallow deer, dark and earthy, with smoked beetroot. Then French cheeses, most of which Joe had never heard of before. Then pear *croustillant* with *crème anglais*. Finally: *digestifs*, coffee, *petits fours*. As the evening wore on, Bastien took an even keener interest in Joe. He didn't seem at all bothered that Wayne was flirting with the older man to his left, dapper in a tartan bowtie and delighted by the American's attention.

After dinner, the revellers began to drift away from the tables. Bastien put an arm round Joe's shoulders. Wayne had left already. 'Where's everyone going?' Joe asked, a little blearily. He was beginning to feel the effects of the *digestif*; its heavy, vanilla-oak flavours had warmed him inside, made his limbs feel looser,

made him feel as if nothing much mattered at all.

'Let me show you.' Bastien's French accent was musical, soft and sensual. Joe followed him down wide stone steps to a large pool. The young men in the water were caught up in tipsy, boisterous horseplay, their shouts and laughter ricocheting around the cavernous space. Others sat idly on deck loungers as if on a steamship bound for warmer seas. Most of them were nude. The older men had chosen not to undress. They watched from the sidelines: the pretty waif-like boys, the handsome muscle men playing in the water.

The pool bar beckoned; at Bastien's request, the barman poured two generous measures of Islay malt.

'This had better be my last.' Joe smiled, trying to keep his words from slurring. 'Or I won't be able to get home tonight.'

'One of my chauffeurs will drive you, just as he brought you here.'

'Do you have a lot of parties like this?'

'*La vie est belle*; life is to be enjoyed; lived as fully and richly as one is able. We owe it to each and every one who is not as fortunate as we are. I like pleasure, I like giving people pleasure. I particularly like giving young men pleasure. It's nice to share in their youth, their exuberance. Are you not enjoying yourself?'

'Yes. Very much.'

'Good. That makes me happy.' Bastien's eyes travelled over Joe's body. Joe liked to be looked at in that way. He liked to be watched and wanted. He imagined the handsome Frenchman's hands on his chest. 'I can see you like to take care of yourself,' Bastien said with a smile. 'I have a state-of-the-art gym I think you'd appreciate.'

Skill mills, Boditrax, kettle bells, TRX and

Wattbikes; every wall mirrored making the room appear even larger than it was.

'I've never seen equipment like this outside a commercial gym,' Joe said.

'You're welcome to use it any time you like.' Bastien reached into his jacket pocket and produced a business card. He pressed it into Joe's palm. 'By the way, are you free on Tuesday evening? My driver will pick you up at seven.'

Joe's head started to swim on the way home. He fought hard to stay awake; he didn't want the chauffeur to think him a young fool. He usually stuck to a couple of glasses of wine with dinner; alcohol and the perfect body did not mix well. He would pay dearly in the morning. Kenny was droning on about the food, the atmosphere, the sexy boys, the New York stock broker who'd asked him out. Joe didn't really know Kenny that well. They'd met a few months before on a cold spring morning at Virgin Active, reaching for the same dumbbells at the same time. They agreed to share the equipment and spot each other. They continued in a similar vein as they worked their way around the circuit. At the end of the session, they decided to meet up once a week and train together. Each had realised the other was gay early on; that sixth sense every gay man has when it comes to finding his tribe. Although Joe didn't find Kenny attractive, he was a good gym-buddy - and now a drinking and partying buddy. And possibly, Joe thought, a route to a better life with a successful older man. A man like Bastien.

*

On Tuesday evening, a black Mercedes was waiting outside as promised. Joe had put on his best suit; the cut emphasised his broad shoulders and compact waist; the soft sheen of the cotton sateen accentuated the heft of his buttocks and thighs. This evening, the destination was The Colony Grill at the Beaumont in Mayfair; Bastien had reserved the private dining room for a candlelit *diner à deux*. To begin: classic New York Shrimp Cocktail. Then butter-soft fillet of beef, dry-aged on the bone, with an accompaniment of *Café de Paris* snails and crisp market garden salad. They drank champagne cocktails as aperitifs then *Gattinara Riserva* with the beef, and a good glass of *Rum St Jacques* with pear and vanilla *rum baba*. Joe was curious about Bastien's relationship with Wayne.

'We have an understanding,' Bastien said with a flicker of a smile. 'He comes and goes as he pleases. He can be quite the loner. I enjoy him when I want to. It works for both of us, for the time being, at least.'

'Has there ever been anyone special?' Joe was fishing.

'I deny myself nothing, and no one. It's good to taste the richness of life, of food and drink, of men and sex. *Tout est bon.* But there'll come a time when I want to settle down, I'm sure. One day. For the right person.'

'You look very good for your years.'

'I am very particular about my diet. I eat only the finest things. I run every morning, and I swim most evenings. I keep my body toned and my mind clear. I meditate.'

The limousine dropped Bastien home first. Bastien kissed Joe and stroked his cheek tenderly before getting out of the car. 'I'm giving a dinner party on Saturday for a few select friends. Say you'll come.'

*

Joe gripped the barbells firmly. He lifted the bar from the rack and raised it until his arms locked. He fixed his gaze on the bright point of the overhead light. Although the air-conditioning was running, the room was still uncomfortably warm. At peak times, it was always too crowded; too many people queueing for too little equipment. Kenny had messaged to say he couldn't train this week: his stockbroker was taking him to New York. The guy clearly liked to move fast, and he clearly liked Kenny. Joe took a deep breath and brought the bar down slowly and smoothly until it rested on his chest. After a moment, he breathed out fiercely, heaved the bar upwards and locked his arms again. He held this position for a couple of seconds before repeating the movement, completing a set of twelve repetitions. He replaced the barbells on the rack and sat up, wiping the back of his neck with his towel. He took a long drink of water, enjoying the coolness as it ran quickly down his throat.

He thought about the large, cool, empty space of Bastien's gym and the offer to use it 'anytime'. He wondered how that would sit with Wayne. He didn't want to tread on anyone's toes, didn't want to make any enemies. Bastien's place was big enough for them both; there'd be no reason to run into each other - unless they wanted to. He wondered about the 'understanding' Bastien had with Wayne. Was he already bored with the kid? Joe didn't want to be just another young, hard body to be played with for a while then tossed aside. On the other hand, his little studio flat was very small and his mortgage very large. Life with Bastien would be colourful and expansive and *luxe*, while it lasted at least. Kenny was already tasting the high life with his

New York City broker. Joe had the feeling Kenny might never come back from the US. Kenny, the stock broker's pet, the resident alien, the naturalised American. Why shouldn't Joe grab a slice of the action too? He'd worked hard enough pumping iron; watching his diet; drinking water, not drinking much else. Why not enjoy the attentions of an older man with a great deal of money? He'd certainly sweated for it. And sweated for it some more. Back in the changing room, he watched the powerful bulk of his thighs flex as he eased off his gym shorts and sweat-dampened briefs. He imagined stripping slowly for Bastien after a hard workout, muscles pumped and burning.

*

The dinner guests were fewer this time, just the older men; Joe was the only young guy at the table. No sign of Wayne. All eyes were on Joe; and he liked it that way. He liked the idea of his flesh being desired. He was an award-winner on Oscar night. Bastien sat at the head of the table; Joe was seated opposite, a little disappointed because he'd hoped to be close and play footsie. For much of the evening, the other guests asked Joe about himself. After a while, it got tiresome, and then it got personal. 'I'm sorry to hear that you've no family,' said Eduardo, a small, wiry industrialist sitting to his left. Eduardo's hair was white but his black eyebrows were neatly plucked and trimmed. He touched Joe lightly on the forearm each time he asked a question.

'I was very young when my parents died,' Joe said. 'And my aunt was very kind to me. She had no kids of her own so, in a way, I was the son she never had.'

'Is she still with us?'

'No. She died last year.'

'That is sad. I bet she doted on you; you must have been an adorable little boy.' He patted Joe lightly on the belly. 'I bet she spoilt you rotten.' Joe smiled at him and gave Bastien a 'rescue me' look. But Bastien was deep in conversation at the other end of the table.

The main course arrived: a delicate sole *meunière* accompanied by several bottles of *Château La Mission Haute Brion* followed by an excellent *chariot de fromages*: *Brie de Meaux Dongé, Caciocavallo Podolico, Beaufort d'Eté*. Joe was beginning to feel the now-familiar effects of too much alcohol when Bastien suggested they retire to the drawing room. Joe was surprised when the other guests didn't join them. He lay back on the sofa as Bastien poured XO into warmed glasses.

'I'd swear you were trying to get me drunk,' Joe mumbled, hands behind his head, biceps flexed, legs spread clumsily to draw Bastien's attention. Bastien sat next to him and walked his fingers slowly along Joe's rock-hard thigh, all the way to the top. Joe felt his heat rising, an almost unanswerable hunger now. He let Bastien unzip him and reach inside; let Bastien take him in his hand; let Bastien knead him while kissing his eyelids, his mouth, his neck. They tore at each other's clothes - shirt buttons, belts, zippers, underwear. Joe's hard body tremored and rose under Bastien's expert touch. He let himself be guided by the older man, urged on, held back, steadied, urged on again, pushed to an inevitable, brutal climax.

They lay by the fire. The burning firewood crackled and spat in the grate. Joe felt Bastien's breath hot against the back of his neck.

'I like having you here in my home. I like your company. Stay with me tonight.'

'What about Wayne?'

'I told you. He and I have an understanding. He is rarely here these days. He spends more time with his college friends than he does with me.'

'So you're all alone here, in this big house?'

'There are the servants, of course. But I like having another man in my bed. I would like to have you in my bed.'

They made love in Bastien's ornate fourposter with its marquetry shield and lion rampant and sheets of fine Irish linen. Joe supposed the bed must be a family heirloom and he wondered what Bastien's ancestors would have made of his choice of bedmate. He had no idea what time their lovemaking ended, but the sky was already growing pale, the night spent.

Bastien pulled him close just as a sharp rap sounded at the door. A maid brought in breakfast on a silver tray: coconut crepes with creamy ricotta and foraged, wild strawberries, freshly squeezed blood orange juice, sweet and zesty, and a pot of strong black coffee. Joe sat at the small table laid for two looking out onto neatly-clipped yew hedges, rhododendrons and espaliered pear trees - all gathered together under a warm, painted sky.

'Do you like it here?' Bastien asked, watching him closely.

'Yes, very much.' Joe smiled.

'Then don't leave. Stay here. With me.'

Joe hesitated. It all seemed too perfect, too much like a dream — or a ridiculous fantasy after too many tequila slammers. One moment he was a junior IT technician struggling to pay his bills, next he was being offered the chance to live in luxury as a kept man. 'What would I do all day?' he asked.

'Anything you like. Work on your physique,

swim in the pool, read books, listen to music, watch movies in the cinema room, join me for breakfast, lunch, and dinner.'

'What about my job?'

'Give it up.'

'My flat? My mortgage?'

'Sell your flat, repay the mortgage. Life is to be lived, Joseph, to be eaten up — see it all, have it all, don't miss a thing — don't you agree?'

'Yes, I do. But when we met, you were with someone else; and he's still part of your life.'

'Less and less now. He is nothing to me compared to you. From the moment I saw you, I knew. You are beautiful in a way I've never experienced before. You are bright; you have so much potential. I can teach you things, guide you to new experiences, show you how to appreciate fine food and wine, music and literature, the ballet, the opera. You'll come to understand the language and loves of the most powerful people in the world; you'll join that world.'

'But I'm just a kid from east London.'

'Not to me. Let me share with you all that I know, let me help you to grow.' Bastien grasped his hand and took him to the window. 'I can give you all this,' he said as he gently stroked Joe's shoulders, kissing the nape of his neck.

'What if you get bored with me one day?' Joe said.

'I know my own mind. I am an intelligent man, a powerful man, Joseph. I know what I want, and I take it.' He turned Joe to face him. His eyes were dazzling blue. 'I give you my word. You need never worry; I will take care of you for the rest of your life. If that's what you want?'

Joe paused for just the right amount of

time: 'It is.'

*

He gazed across the elegant iron-and-glass structure of the Paul Hamlyn Hall. He had grown to love the Royal Opera House with its Italianate facade like a chalk drawing and its tall windows showing gold against the black of night. From their table in the Balconies Restaurant, he watched the people bustling in the bar below, small and insignificant as insects. He scooped up a spoonful of mango and coconut panna cotta, exploring the opposing forces of tart fruit and cream with his tongue. Bastien smiled at him. 'Are you enjoying the performance?'

'I prefer Verdi to be honest. The Italians are lighter and more elegant somehow. Wagner can be a little stark, and way too long.'

'A little too German, no?'

'I never said that,' Joe laughed. 'I did enjoy *The Pearl Fishers* at the ENO.'

'An English translation doesn't always do justice to the work, however.'

'But it's a beautiful French opera whichever language they sing.'

'You've come a long way, *mon chéri*. You've learned so much.'

'All because of you.' Joe took Bastien's hand and kissed it gently.

'The potential was always there inside you. I just helped to bring it out.'

'And now I'm a different man.'

'No, no, you are anything but. You are the man you were always meant to be - intelligent, cultured, sophisticated. *Raffiné*, as we say.'

The five-minute bell sounded. As they rose from the table, Joe couldn't help thinking how handsome they both looked in black tie; and how well they looked together. Just a few months ago, Joe had been a nobody with a wardrobe of nothing but tee shirts, jeans and trainers. The only books he ever read were on the development of muscle tone and proteins for fitness. This afternoon he'd finished reading *Malady of Death*, Marguerite Duras' ruthless meditation on sexual desire — *le petit mort* as the French called orgasm. His life had changed so much in such a short space of time, he was almost a stranger to himself. He kept up his gym routine - most days. Although the rich diet had made him a little fuller in the face. And around the waist. 'Wait!' Bastien said, resting a hand on Joe's arm, then he straightened Joe's bow tie before they walked back into the auditorium, hand in hand.

*

The next morning Joe was feeling guilty, and fat. He left Bastien asleep in bed and hit the basement gym. After the opera, they had gone on to the Wolseley in Piccadilly for espresso martinis. Joe needed to force the toxins from his body. He began at the chest press; he set the incline bench to thirty degrees and grabbed two dumbbells. He leaned back, tucking his elbows in slightly, pushing his arms straight up, controlling the weight for three seconds on the downward movement. After three sets of twelve reps, he could feel his chest firming up, tightening. It felt good to be pumped up, reassuring; a return to power. He dropped the dumbbells to the floor and sat up. Bastien was standing in front of him. 'I have to go out this morning,' he said rather stiffly. 'There are a few preparations for tonight's dinner.'

'Tonight's dinner?' Joe said.

'Didn't I tell you? We are entertaining some friends tonight. The usual guys, you know.'

Joe was sensitive to the awkwardness in Bastien's tone. 'Is everything okay?'

'Everything is fine. Perfect, in fact. I'm just tired after last night; too much champagne, too little sleep.' After a cursory peck on the cheek, Bastien was gone.

Joe spent the next hour building up a sweat, working on his shoulders, pectorals, abdominal muscles and glutes. He always liked to look his best — and his biggest — when Bastien's friends came for dinner. It was usually the same group of older guys, good-looking older guys.

*

Bastien didn't come home for lunch so Joe ate alone. He asked chef for a large tuna tartare.

Then he went down to the library and picked out another Duras; this time, *The Lover*. He spread himself out on the large, weathered Chesterfield in the drawing room. Warm afternoon sunlight fell across his upper body as he turned the pages describing the illicit desire between a schoolgirl and a twenty-something Chinese in French Indochina; his eyelids became heavier and heavier. He woke with a start. It was just after five; enough time for a run to work up an appetite before dinner.

*

He took a quick shower and found his favourite powder blue Ozwald Boateng suit laid out on the bed. Bastien was standing at the window. He turned and smiled at Joe. 'Wear the blue tonight,' he said, clipping a cufflink into place. 'I love you in it.'

'Anything you say.' Joe grinned. He opened a drawer and took out a pair of simple white briefs. Bastien stopped him.

'No,' he said, 'wear nothing underneath.'

Joe kissed him on the cheek and whispered in his ear, 'Anything you say...'

*

The guests always assembled in the drawing room around seven-thirty. Kareem sat down next to Joe. Kareem always sat next to Joe during pre-dinner drinks if he could, always flirted, always touched, and Joe always liked it.

'How do you do it, young man?' Kareem said, squeezing Joe's knee. He was dark, intensely handsome, from an oil-rich Middle Eastern family.

'Do what?' Joe said, playing along with the little game.

'Look even more gorgeous every time I see you.'

'It's a knack.'

Kareem looked bemused.

'A skill,' Joe explained.

'Aaah,' said Kareem, and laughed as he grew bolder and patted the top of Joe's thigh. 'You must keep it up, at all costs.'

Bastien's butler announced dinner. All twelve men filed into the dining room. Joe went to sit next to Bastien but Bastien waved him away, indicating that he should sit at the head of the table. The men stood on either side, watching him more avidly than usual. He felt their eyes on him; he wondered if they could tell he had on no underwear; he felt like a catwalk model, a rock star, a porn star, a god.

'Tonight is a very special night for you, Joseph,' Bastien told him, a playful gleam in his eye. 'Tonight you are the guest of honour.'

The door opened and Joe recognised the American stockbroker, Kenny's ticket to a new life. 'Sorry I'm late, guys,' he said.

'I know you,' Joe said. 'You're dating Kenny, aren't you?' The man looked a little uncomfortable. 'Oh God,' Joe said, 'I'm sorry, I just assumed you were still together. I haven't heard from him in ages.'

'It's fine,' the man said smoothly. 'Kenny was wonderful.'

'I'm sorry it didn't work out,' Joe said.

'It did work out very well. For a while. But it ran its course.'

Joe made a mental note to text Kenny that night; see how he was doing.

Bastien raised his glass: 'To Joseph,' he said and the other men echoed the toast. 'In honour of you, my darling, I have arranged a very special dinner of all your favourite things.' The service began with *langoustine à la nage*, Joe's

first choice whenever he and Bastien dined at the Ritz.

Joe was honoured, proud, excited, and a little self-conscious. He loved surprises: the time Bastien had jetted him away to Nice unexpectedly for a weekend at *Le Negresco*; the time Bastien reserved a suite at the *George Cinq* in Paris and they dined at *Guy Savoy*. Now Joe was feasting on his best-loved dishes from their time together. The fish course was turbot encased in a light mussel mousse - one of the world's loveliest delicacies, Bastien always said. Joe was finishing the last of his *rum baba*, accompanied by a small glass of *Château d'Yquem* when Bastien stood up and asked his guests for quiet. He walked around the table and stood behind Joe, resting his hands lightly on Joe's shoulders.

'It has been such a wonderful time since you came into my life,' he said. Joe looked up, smiling a little foggily. What was the name of the dessert wine? A famous name. It was there on the tip of his tongue. His head was swimming, not unpleasantly. Bastien continued to talk, but Joe couldn't quite keep up. 'You have changed so much,' Bastien said. 'You are bigger physically, which is, of course, wonderful.' The men around the table laughed, someone whooped. 'But you have also developed your mind; you have become something more than *the sum of your parts*. I think that's the idiom, isn't it?' He smiled down at Joe. 'But now, as with all things, the end must come.'

What?

Was he dumping him?

In front of all these people?

Joe tried to sit up, but Bastien's hands were pressing down firmly on his shoulders. 'What do you mean?' Joe said.

His tongue felt thick.

Was he slurring his words?

The men around the table were standing up now, pulling out his chair, grabbing his muscular arms and legs, lifting him bodily onto the table. Crockery and glassware crashed onto the floor. 'Hey get off me!' Joe shouted. 'What's going on?' Were they going to rape him? Was this how it ended — these men taking what they had spent so much time looking at, thinking about, lusting for? His heart was pumping the blood faster round his body. The men wanted him. He knew that. They all wanted him. In spite of himself, his cock twitched, unrestricted by underwear, in the beautifully cut trousers of his suit. One of the waiters returned with something on a silver tray. 'Hey!' Joe shouted to him. 'Help me! Get them off me!' The waiter ignored him, his gaze fixed on Bastien. 'What the fuck's going on?'

Joe began struggling on the table, bucking and kicking in his panic, realising with mounting dread that he could no longer feel his arms and legs.

'It's quite painless,' Bastien smiled as he bent and kissed Joe on his forehead.

'What?' Joe was struggling to breathe; his voice was hollow. 'What are you doing?'

'We've been plumping you up all this time, my love,' Bastien said, 'like a *foie gras* goose on the end of a funnel of maize. We've been filling you physically *and* mentally. The finest meat, the finest music, art and literature. Now you're ready - a magnificent piece of livestock - and we'll each of us benefit from your size, your fullness.'

'You can't —.' Joe's face was wet with tears. 'You're all crazy!'

'No, my love, we are far from that. It's really very simple.' Bastien looked around at the other men. 'We stay vigorous, we stay powerful, gifted, undiminished, by feeding on your flesh, your youth, your life-force.'

'People will wonder where I've gone,' Joe croaked as the room began to spin. 'Kenny, Wayne. Someone will notice. They'll tell the police.'

'No one will ask where you've gone. No one will care. And soon another eager boy will jump into your shoes without a second thought. And he'll have a wonderful life too, for a while — a free-range cock reared to fill the hungry bellies of men.' The other guests began to laugh, a low and sombre kind of laugh; the laugh of men who have seen so much beauty, and so much death. 'And as for Kenny and Wayne,' Bastien said, 'what do you think you've been eating these past few months? The finest and rarest of all meats.' The room fell silent. The men stood back. 'I'm sorry, chéri.

Please believe that I really take no pleasure in this.' Bastien took up the boning knife from the waiter's tray and smiled a dismal smile.

fin

William Jackson

WILLIAM JACKSON IS A BRITISH AUTHOR OF QUEER HORROR FICTION. HIS CHARACTERS INHABIT A HOMONORMATIVE WORLD IN STARK CONTRAST TO THE HETERONORMATIVITY OF SO MUCH HORROR NARRATIVE. HIS WRITING LOOKS AT OPPRESSION, THE INHERENT SEDUCTIVENESS OF EVIL AND THE CORRUPTION, OR MORAL DECAY, OFTEN MASKED BY BEAUTY.

WWW.WILLIAMJACKSON.UK

THE CAMBRIDGE QUEER PRESS PUBLISHES WILLIAM JACKSON'S MAJOR QUEER HORROR WORKS INCLUDING *SATAN'S LAMP*, *THE SUGAR PIT* AND THE SHORT STORY COLLECTION *SHAPES IN THE DARK*

WWW.CAMBRIDGEQUEERPRESS.CO.UK

Cambridge
Queer Press

PUBLISHER'S CHOICE

A COLLECTION OF SLIM VOLUMES
SELECTED BY OUR PUBLISHER

No. 1

THE MIRACLE OF PONT-L'ABBÉ
A SHORT STORY FROM THE COLLECTION
STORIES FOR BOYS
BY BARRY STEWART HUNTER

No. 2

THE FIRST MANIFESTO OF SURREALISM
THE STORY OF YVAN GOLL'S MANIFESTO OF SURREALISM
PUBLISHED 14 DAYS BEFORE ANDRÉ BRETON'S
WITH AN ESSAY BY MARTIN FIRRELL

No. 3

OUT OF WATER
A QUEER HORROR STORY FROM THE COLLECTION
SHAPES IN THE DARK
BY WILLIAM JACKSON

No. 4

150 YEARS OF GERTRUDE STEIN
OUR PUBLISHER'S CHOICE FROM THE SHORT
WORKS OF GERTRUDE STEIN TO MARK
150 YEARS SINCE HER BIRTH

No. 5

ALL THE BEAUTIFUL BOYS
AN ORIGINAL SHORT STORY FROM
THE MASTER OF QUEER BRITISH
HORROR, WILLIAM JACKSON

No. 6

HOW TO WRITE LIKE MRS WOOLF
C. FARR ON HOW A WRITER
MIGHT SET OUT TO CREATE
RATHER THAN IMITATE FORM